Some people say that psychic powers are tricks. In a laboratory the person with psychic powers cannot use their tricks. Other people disagree. We do know that the human brain is very powerful. No computer can do all the things that the human brain can do. Scientists who study the brain think that most people only use some parts of their brains. The other parts are not used in normal life. Perhaps the people who have psychic powers can use these other parts of their brain.

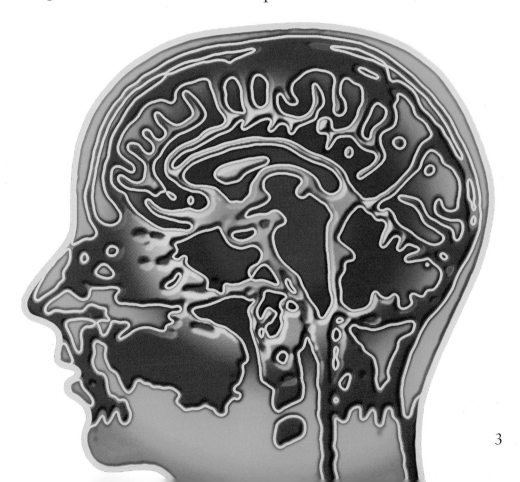

Living again

THE HYPNOTIST

Some people believe that we can live more than once. They think that when someone dies, they return to life as another person in another place and time. This is called **reincarnation**.

Hypnotists sometimes help people remember past lives. It is difficult to know if these are real lives, or if they are just made up.

A British woman called Jane Evans was **hypnotized**. She began talking as if she were another person when she was under hypnosis. The hypnotist asked this other person questions. She said her name was Rebecca and that she lived in York. She said that the King was Richard the Lionheart. Richard was on the throne from 1189 to 1199.

Contents

Introduction 2
Living again 4
The hypnotist 4
Remembering past lives 6
Can people live again? 8
Extra Sensory Perception 10
Psychic spies 12
Can people really use ESP? 14
Seeing the future 16
Disaster warnings 16
Timeslip prediction 20
Can people really see the future? 22
Telekinesis 24
The science of the mind 26
Poltergeists 28
Talking to the spirits 30
The medium and the monks 32
Mystic fraud? 34
Out of body experiences 36
Bizarre powers 38
Electric people 38
Flying people 40
Magic tricks 42
Finding out more 44
Glossary 46
Index 48

Introduction

Some people say they have strange powers. They say that they can predict the future. Or that they know what is happening hundreds of kilometres away. Or that they can fly. Or make objects move just by thinking about it. These kinds of powers are called **psychic powers**. This means that they are powers of the mind.

It's very difficult to test whether these powers are real or a trick. People who say they have psychic powers often can't make them work in a **laboratory**. Many **psychics** say they cannot control exactly when their powers will work. This means it is very difficult to study psychic powers.

'Rebecca' told the hypnotist many things about Medieval York. Jane Evans could have found out most of the things Rebecca talked about, except one. Rebecca was a Jew. There was an

anti-Jewish riot in York. Rebecca said she hid in the burial place, under of St Mary's church, and was killed there. But there was no known burial place under St Mary's.

Then, a few years later, the remains of the burial place were found. Jane Evans couldn't have made this up. Perhaps it really was Rebecca talking.

REMEMBERING PAST LIVES

Sometimes people do not need to be hypnotized to remember past lives. In 1934 a man was walking down Fleet Street in London. A man he had never met before stopped him and said, "I know you." The man looked at the stranger. He suddenly remembered where they had met. "Yes," he said. "I stabbed you and you died." Both men tried to remember what had happened. They decided that they had both been **gladiators** in a Roman arena. They had been forced to fight to the death.

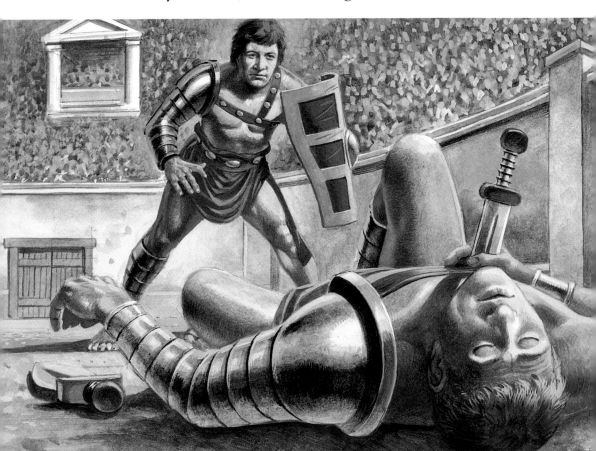

A famous writer called Joan Grant remembered her past lives in her dreams. In 1936 she began remembering a life as an Egyptian princess over 3,000 years ago. She wrote down the memories as if they were a story. The story was published as a book.

One man was frightened of bird feathers. He went to a hypnotist where he remembered a previous life. In the previous life he died as vultures gathered around him. After he had remembered this, he lost his fear of feathers.

CAN PEOPLE LIVE AGAIN?

There are many theories about people who remember past lives. One theory is that people make up the memories to become famous. Or they make up the memories without actually meaning to. For instance, the man frightened of feathers might have made up the story about vultures to explain his odd behaviour.

Both these theories rely on people making up a past life. They would have to use things they had read or seen on TV. But Jane Evans remembered a burial place that no one else knew about.

Hindus believe reincarnation is a fact. The god
Vishnu lived different lives. In each life he had different
powers and skills. Hindus believe that people come
back to earth when they die. If they have lived good
lives they come back to a better life. But if they have
been wicked they come back to a worse life.

Extra Sensory Perception (ESP)

SEEING THE UNSEEABLE

Some people say they can use their minds to see things that are hidden or far away. This power does not use any of the five senses, so it is called **Extra Sensory Perception** or **ESP**.

One of the most famous people with ESP was Pope Pius V. On 7 October 1571 Pope Pius went into a trance in Rome. When he woke up he said he had seen a great battle taking place at sea. He said the fleet with Christian crosses had won. A few days later a message arrived in Rome. A Christian fleet had defeated a Moslem fleet on the same day that the Pope had his vision.

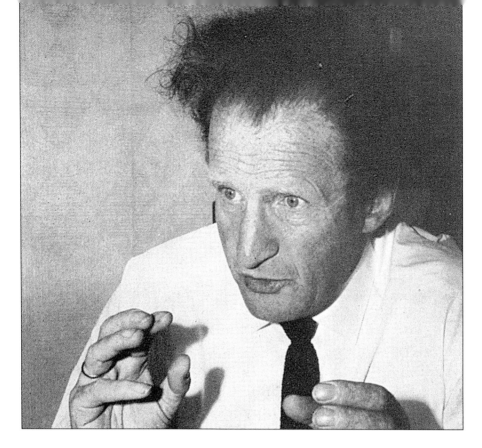

A Dutchman called Gerard Croiset said he could use ESP whenever he wanted. During the 1960s and 1970s he was asked to help find hundreds of missing people. Croiset told one father that his missing daughter was living near a lake. It turned out the girl had argued with her boyfriend. She had gone to stay with a friend near a lake for a few days. Another time Croiset said that a missing boy had fallen in to a canal and drowned near a house with a big weathercock. This also turned out to be true.

PSYCHIC SPIES

Sometimes people with ESP have been used as **spies**. In the 1950s the United States Navy hired some psychics for a secret project. The Navy carried out experiments to discover if psychics could locate enemy ships and aircrafts. The final report said "It looks as if the problem of getting control over ESP has been solved." By 1976 the psychic task force was investigating ways of using psychic power as a weapon. All work since then has been kept secret.

Spy Satellites

Many countries use powerful cameras in **satellites** to take photographs of enemy bases. These cameras can see objects as small as 50 centimetres across. But cameras cannot see inside buildings as people with ESP say they can.

Despite being far out in space, satellites can see their target in great detail.

CAN PEOPLE REALLY USE ESP?

Researchers have studied people with ESP to see what really happens to them. In California during the 1970s, Dr Russell Targ and Harold Puthoff tested a man who said he could read minds. He sat in a room with Dr Targ. Then Dr Puthoff drove a few kilometres away. When Dr Puthoff stopped the car he stared hard at something. The man was asked if he could see what Dr Puthoff was looking at. Many times he described exactly what Dr Puthoff saw.

Dr Carl Sargeant of Cambridge University carried out some experiments in the 1980s. He asked a first person to concentrate on a picture. A second person with ESP sat in another room. This person tried to see the same picture as the first person was looking at. Then he was given four pictures and asked to say which he had seen. If the person chose on chance, he would be right a quarter of the time. But the results showed the person was right nearer a third of the time.

Other experiments have tried to find out if thought waves can travel from one person to another. No trace of any type of energy has ever been found.

Seeing the future

DISASTER WARNINGS

Michel Nostradamus made a lot of **predictions** about disasters. Many people believe his warnings have come true. He lived in France during the 16th century. He predicted several things which came true during his lifetime. Before he died, Nostradamus wrote two books full of predictions.

The ruins of Nagazaki after the atom bomb was dropped

The predictions are very vague. One says that "In two cities near the harbour will be two disasters never seen before." Some people think this predicts the atomic bombs dropped on two Japanese cities in 1945. But it could mean almost anything.

On 20 October 1966 a schoolgirl at Aberfan in Wales had a dream. In the dream her school was destroyed by something black. The next day a giant mass of coal waste slipped down a hill and destroyed the school. A total of 140 people, including the schoolgirl, were killed.

In 1898 a novel was published about a disaster at sea. In the book a **liner** called the Titan hit an iceberg and sank in the North Atlantic Sea. Most of the people on board were killed because there were not enough lifeboats. In 1912 a real liner called the Titanic hit an iceberg and sank. Most of the people on board were killed as there were not enough lifeboats. Had the writer somehow predicted the future?

TIMESLIP PREDICTION

Some people think that it is possible to travel in time for a few seconds and see things which have not happened yet.

During World War 2 an **RAF fighter pilot** was coming in to land at Biggin Hill in Kent. The pilot looked down at the ground. He saw a housing estate he did not recognize. He thought he must be lost. Then he  flew through a cloud. When he looked down again, the houses were gone. The airfield was back where it usually was. Thirty years later the pilot returned to Biggin Hill. He was amazed to see a housing estate exactly where he had seen one before. But this housing estate was real. It had been built a few years earlier. The pilot thought he must have flown through a timeslip. He went into the future for a few seconds and saw the housing estate before it was built.

Philip Lane Photography

The pilot was amazed to see a housing estate on Biggin Hill.

21

CAN PEOPLE REALLY SEE THE FUTURE?

Some people think it is possible to predict the future. If this is true it means that information or people can travel in time. It also means that if something is going to happen, it cannot be changed.

At Aberfan, the coal waste fell because it was unstable. Nobody could have stopped it. But the housing estate which was predicted by the Biggin Hill pilot might never have been built. The land might have been used for a park instead. It is difficult to believe that the future is already decided in this way. Most people believe that the future depends on what they decide to do. They believe that they have some control over their future.

Scientists have studied time a lot. They hope that one day they will find a way to travel in time. Perhaps there is already a natural way for timeslips to happen.

Einstein is famous for his study of time.

Scientists are still trying to learn more about time. Some believe that in certain cases time can pass more slowly. If a star has a strong enough grip on gravity, then it can pull hard at time and slow it down.

Telekinesis

Some people say they can move objects using mind power. This is called **telekinesis,** which means distant movement, or **psychokinesis,** which means mind movement. The power to move objects with the mind is very rare. Only a few people have said they can do it.

One of the most famous people who says that he can use telekinesis is Uri Geller. He became famous in the 1970s. He made metal objects bend and watches stop. He is not the only person to do this kind of thing.

In the 19th century the Italian Eusapia Palladio said she could move tables and chairs around by concentrating on them. She said that she lost weight and got very tired whenever she moved objects. In the early 20th century Stanislawa Tomczyk also could move

Eusapia Palladio

small objects with her mind. However, she gave up doing this in 1919 because her husband didn't like it.

Stanislawa Tomezyk moved objects with her mind.

THE SCIENCE OF THE MIND

One of the most famous cases of telekinesis happened in Russia in the 1970s. It was investigated by scientists. The results may show how telekinesis works.

Nina Kulagina could move small objects just by concentrating on them. She took part in scientific experiments. She was linked to medical monitors and asked to move small objects. When Nina began to concentrate on an object her heart beat rose from about 90 beats per minute to 240 per minute. She also began to sweat. The monitors showed that her brain suddenly worked much harder.

Nina lost weight quickly during the days she was being tested. She often felt dizzy for hours after moving an object. She could not sleep at nights while she was being tested.

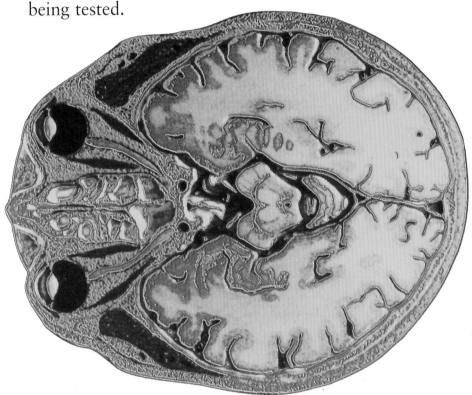

Nina burned up a lot of energy in her brain.

The results show that Nina was under great stress. She was burning up a lot of energy in her brain. Yet it was impossible to pick up any energy passing between her mind and the objects being moved. It is still not known how telekinesis works.

Poltergeists

Perhaps telekinesis can explain some ghostly hauntings. One particular type of ghost, called a **poltergeist**, makes objects fly around a house. Poltergeists usually focus on one person.

A poltergeist will only work when that person is nearby. This is usually a female and fairly young. Often the person is very stressed.

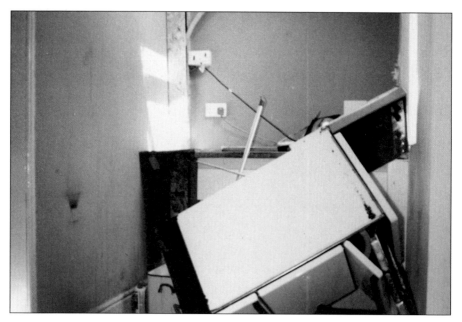

A kitchen damaged by a poltergeist

An artist drew this picture of Philip the poltergeist.

Perhaps poltergeist activity is not a ghost at all. Perhaps the moving objects are caused by the person, using telekinesis, although they don't know it.

In 1974 a group in Canada decided to invent a poltergeist called Philip. The group met several times and concentrated on Philip. Soon the group got some poltergeist activity. Tables moved around and loud thumps were heard. The events only took place when the group was together and concentrating on Philip.

Talking to the spirits

THE MEDIUMS

Some people say that they can talk to the spirits of the dead. These people are called **mediums**. The medium may have a **spirit guide**. This is the spirit of a dead person whom the medium can talk to. The spirit guide passes messages to and from other spirits.

People often visit mediums when their friends or relatives die. They want to ask if the dead person is all right and if there are any messages. The messages usually aren't important. But they mean a great deal to the person who thinks they were talking to a dead relative or friend.

One of the most famous mediums was Doris
Stokes. Doris Stokes said that she could hear the voices
of the dead. She said that they would give her messages
to pass on to other people. Sometimes the messages
were for herself. Doris Stokes often worked in front of a
large audience. She would pass on messages from the
spirits to people in the audience.

Gladys Hayter, the medium, receiving spirit messages

THE MEDIUM AND THE MONKS

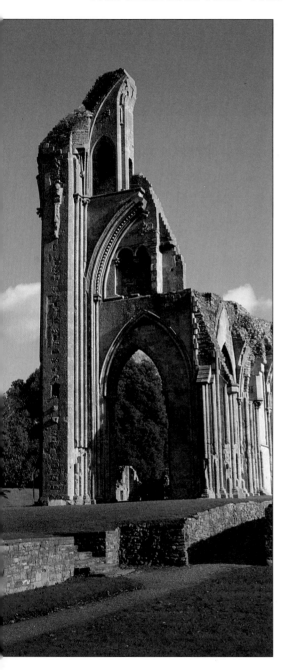

In 1908 Frederick Bond was working at Glastonbury Abbey in Somerset. He was digging up the ruins there. Bond used a medium to help him.

Glastonbury is a very large site. It was important that Bond dug only in the right place. Bond asked a medium named Alleyne Bartlett to help him. The two men talked to the spirits of monks who had once lived at Glastonbury. The spirits told Bond about some buildings which had been destroyed and buried. Bond did what the spirits told him. He found the ruin of a chapel, two towers and several other buildings.

Bond spent ten years digging at Glastonbury. Then he told everyone that his success was due to talking to the monks through a medium. Other messages were passed on by the monk spirits to Bond giving the location of other buildings. No one has dug at Glastonbury Abbey since then.

MYSTIC FRAUD?

Many people think that mediums are not really talking to the spirits. They think that the mediums are either fakes or that they have made a mistake.

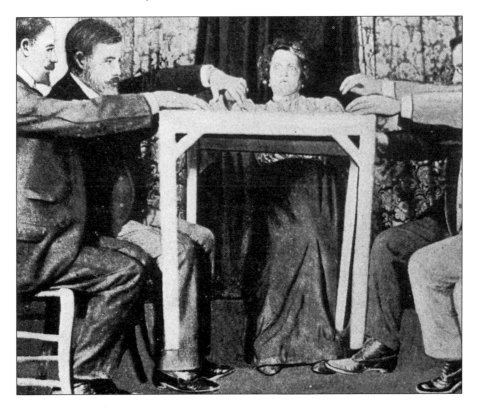

People visit mediums to get messages from the dead. Often these people are very upset because a friend or relative has died. They want to hear from the dead person. They may be easy to trick. A medium who wanted to trick a visitor could find out about a visitor's life before they came. Then when the visitor arrives the medium can say, "Your Uncle Tom has died recently. He has a message." The visitor may be tricked.

During the 1870s a medium called Florence Cook began work in London. She made a lot of money and became famous. Later she confessed that she had used tricks.

Katie King appeared when Florence Cook called her up.

Ectoplasm

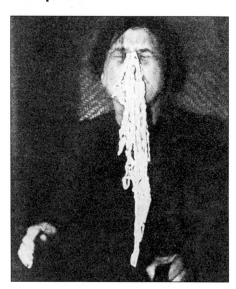

Some mediums claim they can create spirits or objects out of ectoplasm. This is said to be a supernatural substance. When it is produced, it comes out of the ears, mouth or nose of the medium. After a while the ectoplasm might turn into the face of a dead person. However, investigations have shown most ectoplasm is fake.

Out of body experiences

Some people say that their minds have left their bodies for a time. This is known as an **Out of Body Experience,** or **OBE.**

OBEs often happen when a person is ill or unconscious. The person suddenly feels as if they are floating in the air. They usually feel free and happy.

They feel as if they are floating two or three metres in the air. They can see their body quite clearly below them. Usually the OBE ends suddenly as soon as the person realizes what is happening.

Some people think that OBEs are simply very strong dreams. The feelings of floating and happiness are very pleasant. Perhaps a person who is ill will feel better in this type of dream. But some people who have OBEs report seeing things they could not have seen from their bodies. One person reported reading a sign in the next room which she could not have known about.

The OBE saint

St Anthony of Padua is said to have been able to travel outside his body whenever he wanted to. One time he went from one church to another using OBE, so that he could attend a service.

Bizarre powers

ELECTRIC PEOPLE

We all have small electric signals that make our brains and muscles work. But some people seem to have powerful electric signals.

In 1877 in Ontario, Canada, a young woman called Caroline Clare was very ill. When she got better, she found she had unusual powers. Her hands and body seemed to stick to metal objects like a magnet. If she picked up a knife she couldn't put it down again. Somebody would have to pull the knife from her. After four months the magnetic attraction faded.

In 1846 Angelique Cottin from Normandy had the opposite problem. Metal objects would fly away from her touch. Angelique couldn't pick up any metal objects and could eat only with a wooden spoon. After ten weeks the problem faded.

In 1967 Mrs Grace Charlesworth of England noticed that she was getting electric shocks from metal objects in her house. Her husband did not get any shocks at all. The shocks were in fact coming from Mrs Charlesworth. Again, the strange powers faded after a few weeks.

These Russian children have strange magnetic powers.

FLYING PEOPLE

One day in 1650 in Copertino, Italy, a monk named Joseph was at Mass. Suddenly he floated up into the air and drifted forward. He was still deep in prayer. When Joseph reached the altar he bumped into a candle. He yelped in pain and crashed to the floor. Joseph became well known for his odd flights. They only happened when he was deep in prayer. Pope Urban VIII saw Joseph fly. After he died, Joseph was made a saint and called St Joseph of Copertino.

St Joseph is not the only person who has been seen flying. In 1657 a young boy from Shepton Mallet woke up to find himself floating near the ceiling of his room. He floated several times over the following months. Then he stopped.

The most famous flying person was the American Mr Daniel D. Home. Home also said he was a medium. When he tried to talk to the spirits of dead people, Home would sometimes float into the air. Home claimed that over the years he learnt how to control his floating.

Home floating

Many people think that it is impossible to float through the air. They say that stories about people flying are either lies or tricks.

Colin Evans floated in London in 1938.

41

Magic tricks

After World War 1 many people wanted to talk to the spirits of friends and relatives who had died in the fighting. They often went to see mediums. Harry Houdini was a famous stage magician at the time. In 1919 he met a medium whom he thought was a fake. He thought she was making money out of people whose relatives had been killed in the war. He proved she was a fake. Then he began to investigate other psychics.

As Houdini was a very clever stage magician he knew all about tricks.

Houdini shows how luminous faces can be faked

He thought that many mediums were really only good magicians. They used tricks to charge people money for talking to spirits. Houdini visited several mediums to study how they talked to spirits. Then he worked out how to produce all their effects by using tricks and stage props.

Later Houdini learnt how to fake photographs and how to throw his voice as if it were a spirit voice. Houdini investigated several mediums. He proved them all to be fakes, except one.

Houdini shows how ectoplasm can be faked.

Finding out more

Most scientists don't believe in psychic powers. Some people have tried to investigate psychic happenings using scientific methods. Perhaps the most important group is the Society for Psychical Research in London.

The Society was founded in 1882 by a group of scientists and mediums. The first investigations were on ESP and mediums. Later the Society investigated ghosts, telekinetic powers and out of body experiences. The Society tries to investigate strange psychic activity using scientific methods and scientific equipment.

Early members of the Society for Psychical Research

Professor Henry Sidgwick

Sir Oliver Lodge

Sometimes this can be difficult. Scientists who study telekinesis have found that their cameras and electrical equipment keep going wrong. They think that telekinetic power sets up powerful electric fields which makes equipment break down.

The Society has many files and research notes on all types of paranormal activity.

Glossary

ectoplasm A supernatural substance that might come out of the ears, nose or mouth of a medium.

Extra Sensory Perception (ESP) The ability to know what is happening a long distance away.

fighter pilot A pilot of a military aircraft used to destroy other aircraft.

gladiator A person in ancient Rome who fought other people to entertain a crowd.

hypnotize To put a person into a trance. Sometimes in a trance the person can remember past events very clearly.

hypnotist A person able to hypnotize others.

laboratory A room where scientific experiments are carried out.

liner A large ship which carries hundreds of passengers across the seas.

medium A person who claims to be able to communicate with the spirits of the dead.

Out of Body Experience (OBE) The psychic experience of leaving the body and floating free.

poltergeist A type of haunting in which the ghost moves objects around and makes loud noises.

prediction A statement which says what will happen in the future.

psychic A word which means of the mind. It is also used to mean a person who claims to have psychic powers.

psychic powers Powers of the mind which cannot be explained by science.

psychokinesis The power to move an object by brain power alone.

Royal Air Force (RAF) Part of the British government which operates military aircraft, such as fighters.

reincarnation Being reborn in another body.

satellite An object which orbits the Earth in space. Some satellites are used to take photographs of the Earth.

spirit guide A spirit of a dead person said to be used by a medium to pass messages on to other spirits.

spy A person usually employed by the government who discovers secrets to gain secrets about an enemy country.

telekinesis The power to move an object by thought alone.

Vishnu A powerful Hindu god of good.

Index

brain *3, 27*

Cook, Florence *35*

dream *7*

ectoplasm *35, 46*

electric people *38–39*

ESP *10–15, 44, 46*

floating *36, 40, 41*

Geller, Uri *24*

Glastonbury Abbey *32–33*

Grant, Joan *7*

Houdini, Harry *42–43*

hypnosis *4–5*

medium *30–35, 42, 43, 44, 46*

Nostradamus, Michel *16–17*

OBE *36–37, 44, 46*

Philip the poltergeist *29*

poltergeist *28–29, 46*

Pope Pius V *10*

Rebecca *4, 5*

reincarnation *4, 9, 47*

Society For Psychical
Research, The *44*

spirit guide *30, 47*

Stokes, Doris *31*

telekinesis *24–27, 28, 29,
47*

Vishnu *9, 47*